Jirrbal

Rainforest Dreamtime Stories

Maisie (Yarrcali) Barlow

Illustrated by

Michael (Boiyool) Anning

ACKNOWLEDGEMENTS

Thanks to Sandra Gray for giving of her time and effort. Thanks to Michael (Boiyool) Anning for his beautiful illustrations that give my stories life. Thanks to the staff at Magabala Books for having my stories in print so many more can enjoy a part of my culture.

First published in 2001
Reprinted 2002 (twice)
Magabala Books Aboriginal Corporation
2/28 Saville Street
Broome, Western Australia
Email: info@magabala.com
Website: www.magabala.com

Magabala Books receives financial assistance from the Commonwealth Government through the Australia Council, its arts funding and advisory body, and the Aboriginal and Torres Strait Islander Commission. The State of Western Australia has made an investment in this project through ArtsWA.

Printed by Advance Press.
Typesetting and Layout by Red Logic Design, Broome.
Typeset in Goudy 17/26 pt

National Library of Australia
Cataloguing-in-Publication data:

Barlow, Maisie, 1922- .
        Jirrbal, Rainforest Dreamtime Stories.

        For children 7-11 years.
        ISBN 1 875641 06 8.

        1. Aborigines, Australian - Legends - Juvenile literature.
        2. Jirrbal (Australian people). I. Anning, Michael, 1955- .
        II. Title.

398.20994

9781875641031

Contents

The following stories are told by Maisie Barlow, one of the few surviving elders of the Jirrbal people of Ravenshoe, Far North Queensland. The stories are unique in that they reflect a lifestyle which arose from living in the rainforests of the Far North.

The Jirrbalngan developed hunting and gathering techniques which were specific to the rainforest habitat. The Jirrbal people of Ravenshoe occupied a high altitude rainforest. The women developed a time consuming process of leaching poisons from seeds gathered in the rainforest. The men developed unique methods of capturing animals. As the rainforest canopy is the centre of most animal and plant activity, tree-climbing, mastered only by a few, was a necessary and prestigious ability.

Although the Jirrbalngan lived predominantly in the rainforest areas, they also moved at certain times of the year to the drier eucalypt forests and down to the coastal regions. Therefore they had a wide knowledge of differing habitats, and a variety of skills suitable to each area.

Maisie Barlow currently teaches the Jirrbal language and culture in Ravenshoe State School. The stories she tells are those which children in the Jirrbal tribe would hear from their grandparents. As a grandmother and great-grandmother of many children in the school, Maisie is resuming the storytelling tradition, a tradition which was broken with white settlement and the dispossession of people from their land and their families.

Following is a selection of stories which Maisie Barlow tells to the children of Ravenshoe. There are also other stories, which are records of life as it was for Maisie and her family members.

 *Sandra Gray*

The Story of the Narool (Grass), the Gargarra (New Moon) and the Meedin (Possum)

Boiyool ©

Once upon a time on the earth lived the Numorring. They are fairytale people or imaginary people. There was also Narool and Gargarra and lots of others who lived on earth, too.

There were lots of different animals, Yorry , Meedin , Gundoy , Bungurru , Jinjaw , Jargay , Nyargin , Googi and a large variety of Doondoes .

There was plenty of food for all the animals and there was never a shortage of water. Everyone, it seemed, was really satisfied with what they had.

But Gargarra was not. He wanted something different and it was honey.

He asked all the animals if they had any honey. They didn't have any honey but they told Gargarra where he could get some.

"You will have to climb the tallest gum tree in the bush," the animals said, "and there you will find plenty of honey."

So Gargarra found the big tree, but realised that he could not climb it because he was just a new moon. Gargarra thought to himself that he needed someone to help. As he turned around, he saw Meedin  coming his way.

3

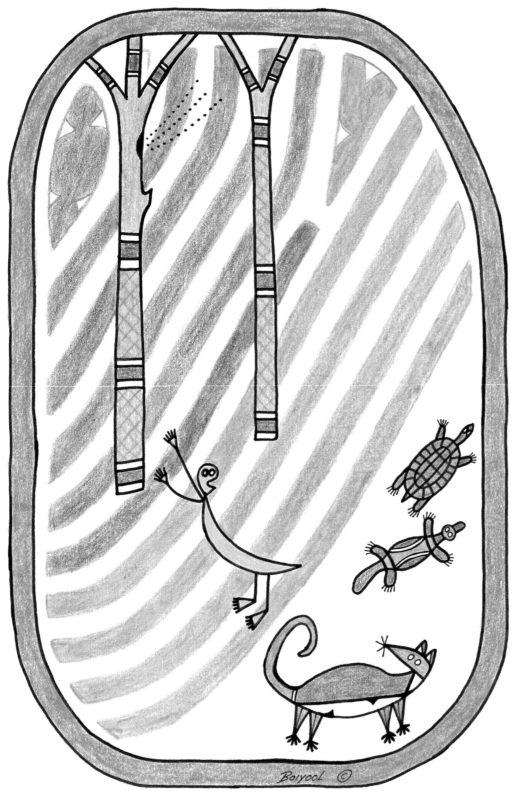

He called, "Hello, Meedin , can you help me get some honey from this tree, as I am very hungry and cannot climb this great big gum tree myself."

But Meedin was on his way to get his own breakfast. "Sorry, old moon, I mean, new moon, you will have to climb up yourself and get your own breakfast, too."

"Oh, well, thank you anyway, Meedin," said Gargarra, "maybe someone else will help."

Many more animals passed by but no one wanted to climb up the big gum tree and Gargarra began feeling very, very hungry. He was so hungry that he decided he would have to be brave and climb the tree himself.

Yorry , Gundoy , Gungargar and the other animals warned Gargarra to be very careful. The bees work very hard to gather up honey from all the other trees that are blooming in spring, because in the wintertime they stay in their hives with enough honey, that they gathered in spring, to last until next spring. So it will be only natural that they would put up a fight if just anybody tried to take and eat their honey.

Despite the warning, Gargarra boldly climbed the big tree and ate most of the bees' honey. While he was fighting the bees off, he kept eating their honey.

BoiyooL ©

But on his way down, he became stuck. He had broken both his legs and was in a lot of pain. He was scared.

He called out for help from the Nyargin  and the group of animals that were watching from below, but no one could help poor Gargarra.

6

So, Meedin ran quickly to Narool  who lived out on the plains. "Come quickly, please Narool, Gargarra is stuck in a great big gum tree. He has broken both his legs and needs help."

Firstly, Narool gathered some blue-top. "What is that?" said Meedin, the possum. "Boobool," said the grass. "Why are you getting it?" said Meedin. "Don't you know what boobool is for?" said Narool to the grass, "It's medicine, for his legs."

Then Narool came fast to climb the tree and help poor Gargarra down.

After helping Gargarra down, Narool and Meedin cleaned his face of all the honey he had eaten. Then he put on the boobool medicine. But blue-top was not enough to heal Gargarra's legs and eventually he lost them.

Soon it was time for Gargarra to journey back home. "I had a lovely time with you all and thank you for all your help. I will shine brightly in the sky at night for you all. But for you, dear Narool, I will send dew at night for you to drink."

So one night, Narool was looking up at the sky and what a sight! There was Gargarra shining down on him and sending dew as he promised Narool he would.

And that is why the grass is wet at night. The new moon is keeping his promise of giving the grass a drink by sending down dew.

If we are also like Meedin and Narool, being kind and helpful, we too may be rewarded kindly.

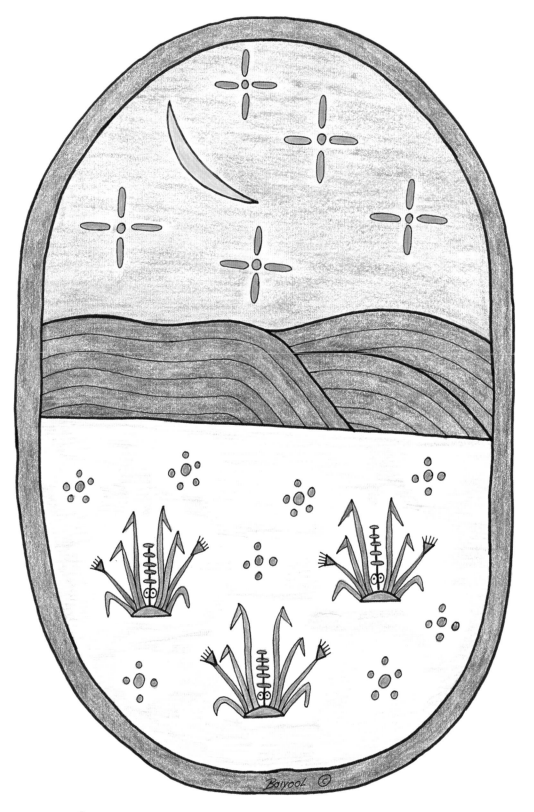

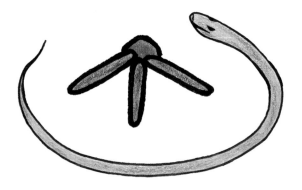

A long time ago in Jujaba time, no animals had any fire to cook with except for Walguy, the brown snake. He was selfish and wouldn't share his buni (fire), with any of the other animals.

All the birds were sick of eating raw food. Grubs and insects were all raw. It was making them feel ill. Gurijala, the eagle-hawk and the birds watched Walguy making his camp high up on the mountain in a cave. He was curled up around his buni, guarding it, and his fire-stick, which is also called a buni.

Jiggiti Jiggiti, the wagtail, looked up at Walguy and asked "Where's our buni?"

Walguy replied, "Try that fire-stick over there." He pointed to an old stick but it was not from the Moreton Bay Ash tree.

And try as hard as he might, Jiggiti Jiggiti couldn't start a fire. The old stick would not make fire like the Moreton Bay Ash fire-stick  would.

Gurijala, the eagle-hawk called all the birds together to think of a way to get some of the buni from Walguy.

Now in Jujaba time, all the birds were the one colour. Gurijala suggested that they paint themselves with yellow clay, so they wouldn't be seen in the sky flying above Walguy.

13

First to try was Bilmbiran, the king parrot. With his wings painted yellow, he disappeared from sight. But when he swooped down to grab some buni, Walguy reared up his head and frightened Bilmbiran off.

Bilmbiran said, "It's your turn now," to Marjatar, the night heron and Guguwun the brown pigeon, who flew up with their wings painted yellow. But Walguy was angry and struck at them, frightening them off.

So the birds all got together again and thought about how to get the buni. "We know", they said, "let's get some birds to sneak up along the ground and steal the coals. Perhaps Walguy won't see us."

First to try was Mungarra , the scrub turkey, who crept up very quietly to the fireside. But Walguy saw him and flicked his tail, covering him with hot coals, and scrub turkey got burnt all over. Maybe Mungarra was too big and so little finch darted in quickly to grab a coal. He was also burnt.

Lastly, Bubunba , the coucal pheasant, and Gugula the flycatcher finch tried, but Walguy was very angry and they both got burnt, too.

Then the white cockatoo, Gayambula, thought, if they were painted with white that it might be a good camouflage. So white cockatoo got painted with clay and flew right up and swooped down, but he was a noisy flyer and Walguy saw him and frightened him away.

They thought again and Gidlila, black cockatoo, said, "If we were all painted with charcoal, he mightn't see us in his camp." So Gidlila and Jawa Jawa, the magpie, tried black. They tried to dive head-down into his camp, but Walguy saw them and they couldn't get near the fire.

Gurijala, the eaglehawk, called all the birds together and, this time, they thought really hard. How can we get the buni from Walguy? They needed someone who could fly very swiftly, silently. Someone who was well camouflaged and tricky.

Jawa Jawa decided to call on Bajinjila, the spangled drongo.

And they painted him up all beautiful and satin black and Bajinjila who was an excellent flier, flew right up high in the sky; so far up that he couldn't be seen anymore.

Then he prepared himself to dive, and silently and swiftly, he dropped from a great height, directly down into Walguy's camp and caught Walguy by surprise—and grabbed hold of the fire-stick.

Walguy was furious and snapped at Bajinjila and caught his tail feathers in the middle, and split them, but Bajinjila flew hard and onto a mountain peak. Bajinjila rested on the mountain peak and Walguy rose up in all his might and struck out in great anger at Bajinjila, who quickly took off. Walguy came crashing down on the peak and split it in two,

which can be seen today near the community of Murray Upper and they call it Split Rock.

So after that, Bajinjila shared the fire among the birds to cook their food on. Walguy crept down into the mountain where he still lives.

That is why the birds have many different colours, from their attempts to steal Walguy's fire.

Bajinjila, the spangled drongo, still has his satin black feathers and fish tail, where Walguy snatched his feathers. He is still very nervous when he lands on a branch. He looks around and flicks his feathers and maybe he is keeping his eye over his shoulder for Walguy.

Fishing Story
About Us

A story of being obedient

Once, long ago, Nguma (father) and Yabu (mother) wanted to go fishing. It was garringa (daytime) and the garri (sun) was shining all over the bugan (forest). They wanted to go fishing in the wabu (scrub), a long way from their mija (camp). The children Yarra and Garjin could not go with them, they had to sit in the mi-mi (children's cubby house).

Their Nguma told them to sit quietly and not call out to anyone or answer anyone. They then set off for the day.

While they were away, the ngalgas (children) played as children will. The garri shone on their mandalany, their children's games...

They became hot and thirsty.

Little Garjin wanted her Yabu (mother). She called, "Yabu, Yabu, Yalubi."

Many times she called until her jurgay (brother) told her to be quiet and remember what their Nguma had told them.

But his jaman (sister), the little Garjin, did not listen to her jurgay. She kept calling for her Yabu. At last she heard a voice answering her cries. She called again, "Yabu, Yabu, Ngaliji baniny." Again she called and again they heard the voice answering, "We are coming."

Yarra started thinking:
the voices are different to the sound of my parents' voices.

He wanted to see who was calling. So he climbed a very tall yugu (tree). He climbed to the very top of the yugu. From there, he could see all around. Little Garjin climbed only halfway as she was too scared to go higher.

Yarra saw the Goy and Gwingan coming towards them. He knew that they were bad, so he kept very quiet and tried to tell his jaman to climb higher in the tree. But little Gargin was too excited to listen—still thinking that they were her parents coming from fishing.

When the Goy and Gwingan arrived at the foot of the yugul, they saw Garjin half way up the tree, nestled in the branches. She realised her mistake, but it was too late.

Both Goy and Gwingan saw her at the same time and both wanted to eat her. They had an argument as to who should eat little Garjin.

The Gwingan shouted that it was her turn to eat, as Goy had eaten the last little naughty boy. The Goy said he must eat her because he was bigger and needed more food.

In the end, Goy reached up and pulled Garjin from her branch. He swallowed her whole and walked away with the furious rantings of Gwingan ringing in his manga (ears). He was so full that he climbed into a hollow tree and went to sleep.

Yarra was so frightened that he stayed in the top of his tree and watched the pair leave in different directions. All the rest of the day, he waited until he saw his parents return.

When his Nguma called him, he didn't answer because he thought that Gwingan had come back to eat him. It wasn't until he actually saw his parents at the foot of the tree that he dared come down off his perch. He told his parents the whole sad tale.

His Nguma was very angry.
He took his axe and went to the
hollow tree and cut around the base
of the tree so that he could pull the
Goy out of his bed.

Nguma split Goy down his bamba (stomach). He pulled his daughter out very gently. He knew little Gargin was frightened, so he told her to go and bathe in the river.

Then he chopped up the Goy and threw the pieces for many miles.

After that, he talked to his ngalgas for a long time. He told them that they must always do as they are told or next time he might not be around to save them.

This story was told widely by parents to instil obedience or fear into their children. In this way, the children learned always to do as they were told by their elders. This obedience carried through until they themselves became elders and passed down the stories.

The Water Story

Once in Jujaba time (the time of Creation) all the people were animals. The blue tongue lizard (Bangarra) had the only water in the world. Bangarra was a very sly creature. He hid his water under a large flat stone. All of the other animals had to chew kangaroo grass (gulbira) if they were thirsty.

One day the animals asked Bangarra for some water. Bangarra replied, "Oh, I haven't got any water. You will have to chew gulbira if you are thirsty. That's what I have to do."

The animals didn't believe him, as he had a wet moustache. "You have a wet moustache," they cried, "You must have water hidden somewhere."

Bangarra just turned his back on them, grunted and walked away.

The animals decided it was time to find out where sly Bangarra had his water hidden. The short-nosed bandicoot was the first animal that tried to follow Bangarra, but the sly lizard saw him and went off in another direction. He didn't want the animals to find where he kept his water.

The possum tried to follow him as well, but Bangarra saw him and again went in another direction.

Then Galu, the tiny mouse, who was the smallest animal of them all, decided to follow Bangarra. Galu, the mouse, crept up behind Bangarra and hid on the right side of his tail.

Bangarra was now very cautious. He looked to the left. Nothing there.

Then, he looked to the right.
Quickly, Galu the little mouse
hopped over to the left side of
Bangarra's tail so he wouldn't
be seen.

Bangarra could not see
him so he continued on his way
towards his water.

Finally, Bangarra came to his secret place where he kept his water. He gently eased a flat stone to one side and began to drink.

Çalu, the mouse, then sprang out from behind Bangarra and tipped the stone all the way off the water. "Wonderful, wonderful, wonderful!" he squealed with joy. "Here is enough water for all of us."

Upon hearing Galu's squeals,
the swallow flew to the spot,
swooped low and gathered water
up in its beak.

The swallow then flew low over the country, spilling the water from its beak. The water from the swallow's beak fell onto the land to make rivers, creeks and lakes as we know them today.

As for Bangarra, his selfishness got him nowhere. In the end, his water was found and now he has to share.

So always share things. No good ever comes of keeping something to yourself. Always share what you have with others and you will always have friends and always be happy.

The stone under which Bangarra kept his water hidden can still be seen to this day. It is on the Atherton Tablelands in far North Queensland.

Learn a Little Jirrbal

Jirrbal is a name derived from the Djirbalngan coastal and rainforest people
south of Cairns in north eastern Australia.
Here are the traditional language words used in this book:

Jirrbal to English

bajinjila
spangled drongo

bamba
stomach

bangarra
blue-tongued skink

bilbaram
King parrot

boobiny
leaden flycatcher finch

boobool
blue-top, billy-goat weed

bubunba
pheasant coucal

bungurru
freshwater turtle

buni
fire

doondoes
all birds

gargarra
moon

garri
sun

garringa
daytime

gayambula
white cockatoo

gidlila
red-tailed black cockatoo

googi
flying fox/fruit bat

gugula
platypus

guguwan
brown cuckoo dove

gulbira
kangaroo grass

gulu
hopping mouse

gundoy
cassowary

gurijala
brown goshawk

jaman
sister

jargay
goanna

jawa jawa
magpie

jiggiti jiggiti
willie wagtail

jinjaw
glider possum

jujaba
Creation time

jurgay
brother

wabu
bush, woodland

walguy
brown snake

mandalany
children's games

manga
ears

marjatar
night heron

meedin
possum

mija
camp

mi-mi
children's cubby house

mungarra
brush turkey

narool
grass

ngarrul
shelter

nguma
father

nyargin
echidna

yabu
mother

yarra
son

yorry
kangaroo

yugu/yugul
tree

English to Jirrbal

birds (all)
doondoes

blue-tongued skink
bangarra

blue-top, billy-goat weed
boobool

brother
jurgay

brown cuckoo dove
guguwan

brown snake
walguy

brush turkey
mungarra

bushland
wabu

games (children's)
mandalany

glider possum
jinjaw

goanna
jargay

grass
narool

camp
mija

cassowary
gundoy

cockatoo, black, red-tailed
gidlila

cockatoo, white
gayambula

creation time
jujaba

hopping mouse
gulu

pheasant
bubunba

platypus
gugula

possum
meedin

kangaroo
yorry

kangaroo grass
gulbira

king parrot
bilbaram

magpie
jawa jawa

moon
Gargarra

mother
yabu

night heron
marjatar

shelter, boughshade
ngarrul

sister
jaman

son
yarra

spangled drongo
bajinjila

stomach
bamba

sun
garri

tree
yugu/yugul

daytime, daylight
garringa

eagle hawk
gurijala

ears
manga

echidna
nyargin

father
nguma

fire
buni

flycatcher, leaden
booniny

flying fox/fruit bat
googi

freshwater turtle
bungurru

willie wagtail
jiggiti jiggiti

Growing up in Ravenshoe

Up in the Tablelands, in a little place called Cedar Creek (now called Ravenshoe) I was born in 1922. My mother named me Maisie. She almost called me May which I liked. May became my pet name.

We were living then out of town, in a place called Bellamay. We had lived there as long as I can remember, until one day the farmer said that we had to move away from Bellamay. So, we moved to Millstream. We had a village there. I was about six or seven then.

When I was young we had to hunt for food. We loved going fishing and cooking it on an open fire, as it tasted very nice. Sometimes we'd go hunting for wallabies to eat. Sometimes we just stayed at home or went swimming. Our grandparents were never sick. They were very healthy people because they lived off the land. The food that they gathered they ate on the same day and nothing was left to go bad.

Just Rewards

One day when my mother came home from work after she got paid, we bought corned meat and Mum wanted a cabbage to go with the corned meat. So she sent my brother and myself to the vegetable garden to buy one cabbage to cook for tea. My brother was only young then. He wanted to pick some of the grapes as we walked along the long path next to the river. I told him that he shouldn't as this was stealing and we mustn't do it. We could see the rows of grapes as we walked and there seemed to be so many, but we didn't take one.

Old George Lee, the owner of the vegetable garden, must have been watching us as we came and he saw that we didn't take any of the grapes. We gave Old George one shilling for one cabbage. He gave us lots more vegetables. He gave us a couple of nice big turnips, a couple of nice big carrots, and tomatoes. I told him that I did not have enough money to buy all these vegetables. He said that he had seen us, and that we were good children, so we could have the vegetables. Then he walked with us up to the grape vines and gave us four big bunches! I said to my brother, "See what happens when you don't touch things that don't belong to you. You get rewarded for being honest."

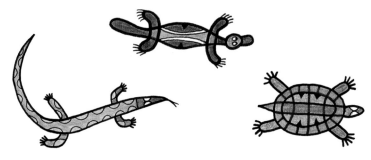

The Family Home

Our house was made from flattened out kerosene tins. It was very big. Roofing iron was on top — and the floor was made from ant bed. The ant beds were cut with an axe in squares and then they were laid on the ground like bricks. They were then wetted and smoothed over. The ant bed flooring went very, very hard.

We slept on fresh bladey grass which we gathered about once a week. The fresh grass was put on top of the old grass then covered with opened out corn sacks. We then put blankets on top. We never lived in the bedroom made for us because it was too far from the fire. Our grandparents had their own room and a fire because they were old and got cold easily.

We did our cooking at the main fire. The smoke went out the door and windows, sometimes it got a bit smoky in there and my eyes used to hurt.

All the water we had to collect at the creek. I was the eldest at home so I had a big minty tin in which to collect water. The younger ones had a smaller tin each. We could not afford to get billy cans. We carried the water back to the house and put it into a big kerosene tin at home.

Childhood Work

Most of the time I used to wear Mum's old clothes. She could never afford to buy us new clothes and where she worked they used to give her old clothes. They were always too big, but they were warm. Mum worked at a white person's house, her name was Mrs Muir. She was a lovely old lady and a widow when we went there. Mum also helped Rose Muir to clean the school. I went along once to see the school because I was not allowed to go to school. I must have been about six at the time. I was told that I was not allowed to go because the white people did not want me to mix with their children. I had always wanted to go to that school and learn to read and write like the white children.

My mother worked every day except Sundays. I used to work at home. I had to do all the housework. Mum brought home tea and sugar and bread. She used to get five shillings a week and we bought meat and some soup bones and we used to eat just that, unless we went hunting. My father worked for Vincent Lee (George Lee the vegetable gardener's nephew). He got 10 shillings a week. He helped run the shop and the little garden.

We used to catch brown frogs from down the river. We had those for lunch when Mum was away all day. We used to throw them over the hot coals. When they burst, we cleaned all their belly out and ate the rest. We also used to eat the watercress out of the river. We threw that over the hot coals too. It was lovely to eat when we were hungry. Frog is really lovely to eat. It has more flavour than chicken and has a nice smell.

Pets

When Marge Brooks and I were about six, Marge's grandparents' dog had a litter of pups. First Grandpa asked Marge if she wanted the black or the white puppy, as she had to have the best one out of the litter because her grandfather was the king of the tribe. She wanted the black one. I too wanted him as he was the smallest, but it was not to be. I had to settle with the white one that was given to me.

About two weeks after we were given our pups the little black puppy crawled into the open fire and burned all his coat off. He looked so ugly that Marge then decided she wanted my white puppy. I gave her my white puppy and I got the black puppy. He did not look very nice but I had him to keep, so I looked after him. I named him Blacky.

One day when Blacky had grown up he looked so lovely with all his coat again that Marge wanted him back. She told me that it was her dog in the first place and that she must have it. I was not going to let her take him off me again though, and so he remained my dog.

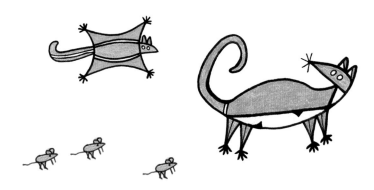

Walkabout

About December we had to go down to Tully for a fight and Corroborree. Of course every family had to take their pets with them. So we had our pets with us as we travelled through rainforest, creeks and rivers. We even travelled through floods. We had no tents, so we slept out in the open and went fishing and hunting. On the way down, all the older children had to help their mothers with the work and the cooking. We had no time to play. There were about one hundred of us travelling down and it took us two weeks to get to the coast.

Everyone carried their own load. Sometimes it was difficult to lift or carry things because they were heavy. The dilly bags were full—some with babies, some with pots and other items, and others with large stones the old ladies used to crush the food. They were so heavy I don't know how the old ladies could carry them. They put the handles of the dilly bags across their foreheads and the dilly bags down their back.

Finally we arrived in Tully late one afternoon. We ate and went to bed. Next day was a big day for everyone. It was a time to settle their differences. When the fighting was over the Corroborree started.

After the Corroborree everyone had a feast. It went on for two weeks. Then the time came to go home. Everyone was saying their goodbyes, except our family, because I was in Tully Hospital. My leg had got cut on a large knife. The cut was very deep and the cut went bad.

We stayed on for five or six weeks. Then one day when the leg was on the mend, we started on our way home.

When we started travelling home we had some food but when the food ran out we had to live off the land. We made our way home by way of the river, so we got lots of fish. On one occasion our father blew up one deep hole and we got lots of fish. My sister and I tried to get a big fish that was floating in the water. We threw some sticks and stones to make a big wave so the fish might come closer to the bank and we could then reach out and get the fish. We were still too far from it to reach it though.

All this time my dog, now fully grown, sat looking on. Suddenly he dived into the river and got the fish in his mouth. He brought the fish in and put it at our feet. After doing that, I told myself that I would never part with him.

Climbing the mountain range was very tiring. On the way up, we ran into three men. Two were white men and one was an old Aboriginal man. He was helping the two white men to trap big pythons. They had the snake skins pinned down on logs to cure them. They were going to sell the skins so that handbags and shoes could be made out of them. We asked them for some food. They gave us tea, sugar and bread. We gave them cassowary meat. We stayed one night close by these men. Next morning we were up at about six o'clock. After eating we went on our way up to the top of the mountain. We were happy as it was bringing us close to home.

When we arrived back in Ravenshoe everybody was happy to see us back again. My elder sister had to go back to work, we saw her only on Sundays. Mum and Dad had to work everyday and come home at 5.00 pm. So I had to take care of my baby sister and brother. I had to look after them all day and of course my very own dog—Blacky. We were very happy those days. All the children were happy to see us. We played and went swimming and had games. We didn't go to school though, so we just stayed at home.

Life on a Cattle Station

When we were school age we never went to school. I always wondered why. Maybe all the mothers in Ravenshoe did not want black children going to school with their children. Yet, when the black children grew up to be teenagers, all the mothers of Ravenshoe town wanted girls to work for them. I told myself I'd never work for them, and I didn't as I was sent out to the cattle station. I grew up on this cattle station. It was lovely out there and I was happy. Also I had my Aunty Dinna. She was with her husband who also worked on the station. So we went fishing. Sometimes we went fishing on horseback. That was in December 1929. Also my Uncle Cormboo and his wife Molly and their little girl Ida were on the same station. I was glad.

The station we were on was Wairuna. It was owned by Mr and Mrs K. Atkinson. They had three little boys so I became their nurse girl. I had to bathe them and feed them. We worked every day in the morning and we had afternoons off from 1.00 to 5.00. At 5.00 we had to start work again. There was one cook, her name was Nora. She was very old but a very good cook. She made nice bread and cooked nice meals. We all had Sundays off too. We had good times, all of us. We were on the station for 8 years. By then the two older boys were school age. So Mrs K. taught her boys school. Mrs. K. asked if I'd like to sit in too, so for that year I did sit in and I loved learning to read and write.

When the children of Mrs. K. were small, all the family had to go down to Cairns or down to Sydney and I had to go with them to take care of the boys. As they grew older and could bathe themselves I didn't have to go anywhere, as I had to look after the station. There was another cook — Mrs. Janken, and a young girl, her name was Cheepa, her brother Dane (a cowboy) and myself. As everybody had gone on the holiday I had the job of looking after a very valuable stallion. I had to look after him, feed him, take him to the night paddock to graze on grass and in the afternoon he had to be put back in his stable as he had to be fed on boiled corn. He was a grey horse. His name was Grey Amber.

One day I let him out in the night paddock and he saw some mares in the other paddock. He started galloping up and down, and I was thinking he might jump over the fence and cut his legs. As he was a valuable horse I had to do something about it. I wanted to take him back to his stables again. The cook kept calling me, telling me to hurry up and do something as she could see from the house what was happening. I went to him and tried to get him to the stable. He kept running up and down the fence. So finally I stood in front of him. He jumped right over me. Again I stood in front of him and again he jumped right over me, just missing hitting me on the head. So, I threw myself on the ground and I lay there as he passed me. He looked back to me and then put his nose on my head. Maybe he was thinking that he had hurt me. He was standing over me so I got up. As I was in a hurry to get him back to the stable I forgot to bring a halter, so I climbed up on his back and he walked back to the stable. I brushed him and fed him and gave him water. Then I gave him a big hug.

Yarrcali, Maisie Barlow

FROM THE AUTHOR:

Living in the bush is so lovely and healthy.
Once a year everybody went into town to do their shopping,
and then back home again. Country life is the best.
That is why we Aboriginal people like to go walkabout,
and to keep fit and well. So if anyone wants to keep well,
go on a walkabout.

ABOUT THE ILLUSTRATOR:

Michael (Boiyool) Anning is a craftsperson immersed in the traditional culture of the rainforest people of the coastal area of north Queensland. By listening to stories from his grandmother and elders of the Nyudgunji tribe (often referred to as Jirrbal speakers), as a young man Boiyool learnt how spears, stone axes, knives, baskets, shields and swords were the instruments of rainforest life.

He now makes and paints traditional and contemporary art objects with natural pigments and charcoal, mainly focussing on large wooden shields and swords of his people, the Ydinji, whose lands were from Cairns, and southwards. In doing so, he hopes to create a broader view of all rainforest tribes and culture.

In 1998 Boiyool became the first Queenslander to win a major prize at the National Aboriginal and Torres Strait Islander Art Awards in the Northern Territory. His work is represented in galleries and touring collections, including the ANU Canberra School of Art Gallery.

Boiyool is the name of a legendary part-man, part-eel, creature in Ydinji folklore and was given to him by his great-aunt, a Ydinji tribe member.

Boiyool, Michael Anning